E WON
Wong, Janet S.
The trip back home
31856013538952

DEMCO

THE TRIP BACK HOME

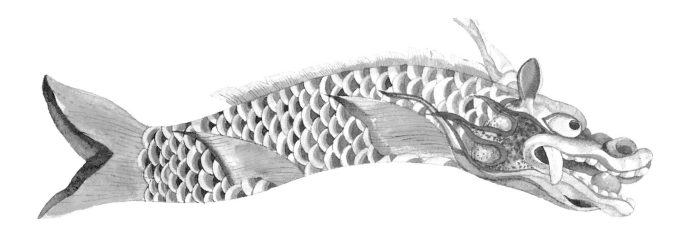

WRITTEN BY

Janet S. Wong

ILLUSTRATED BY

Bo Jia

Harcourt, Inc.

Orlando Austin New York San Diego Toronto London

Requests for permission to make copies of any part of the work should be submitted
online at www.harcourt.com/contact or mailed to the following address:
Permissions Department, Harcourt, Inc.,
6277 Sea Harbor Drive, Orlando, Florida 32887-6777.

www.HarcourtBooks.com

Library of Congress Cataloging-in-Publication Data
Wong, Janet S.
The trip back home/written by Janet S. Wong; illustrated by Bo Jia.
p.   cm.
Summary: A young girl and her mother travel to Korea to
visit their extended family.
[1. Family life—Korea—Fiction.   2. Korea—Fiction.
3. Korean Americans—Fiction.]   I. Jia, Bo, 1962–   ill.   II. Title.
PZ7.W842115Tr   2000
[E]—dc21   97-9692
ISBN 978-0-15-200784-3

G I K M N L J H F

Printed in Singapore

The illustrations in this book were painted
with watercolors on 300 lb. Arches watercolor paper.
The display type was hand-lettered by Georgia Deaver.
The text type was set in Weiss.
Printed and bound by Tien Wah Press, Singapore
Production supervision by Pascha Gerlinger
Designed by Lori McThomas Buley

In honor of Halmoni, Haraboji, and Imo—
and my mother, who took me to meet them
on our trip back home

—J. S. W.

To Olivia Yi and Hugh Dao

—B. J.

The week we went on the trip back home
to visit the village where Mother grew up,
we shopped for gifts for our family,
things we thought they would need.

Then, in our brand-new traveling clothes,
we flew a day and a night and a day,
wiping our faces awake with hot towels
when we arrived in Korea.

We gave my grandfather, my *haraboji*,
a pair of leather work gloves,
tough and tanned
like his thick-skinned farmer's hands.

We gave my grandmother, my *halmoni*,
an apron, ruffled at the edge,
with two large pockets
in the shape of flowers.

We gave my aunt, my *imo*,
a picture book with simple words
to teach her English.

They gave us hugs.

Every morning
before the birds began to sing,
Haraboji woke me up
so I could watch him
push a fresh block of charcoal
into a tunnel near the house.
The charcoal sat smoldering on stones,
warming the air under the floor
while Mother slept late
those cold autumn mornings.

And always, every morning,
Haraboji let me wear his new leather gloves,
good for grabbing the charcoal
he made from stumps of trees.

Every day
before shopping with Halmoni,
I fed the hungry pigs
scraps of carrot and onion and egg
I rolled with rice.
I threw the sticky balls
as hard and as fast and as far as I could
so the running pigs would not
knock me down.

Then Halmoni and I walked
up the rough dirt road to the outdoor market.
We searched through rows of tiny stalls
filled with clouds of rice cakes
and rivers of small soup fish
and hills of hot chili peppers,
searching for something crispy, fresh,
and cheap enough for five.

Back at the house
Halmoni made a fire in the stove
with pine branches I gathered.
Into a heavy iron pot
she measured the rice with a silver bowl
and I washed the rice
while she floated black sheets of seaweed
back and forth over an open flame
until the black turned to green.

Mother pulled spicy *kim chi* cabbage
from a cool clay jar
and set soup on the stove
to simmer.
Imo mixed mung bean sprouts
with sesame oil and sesame seeds
and garlic she had smashed
with a stone.

After we ate
Halmoni and Mother and Imo and I
would sit in the afternoon sun,
sewing warm clothes for winter,
while Haraboji crouched on the roof,
sandwiching persimmons in straw,
where they would be stored
all autumn.

And always, every day,
Halmoni let me wear her new ruffled apron,
good for holding spools of thread
and even better for hiding persimmons.

Every evening
before we unfolded our soft cotton beds,
we sat in a circle
on the smooth, warm *changpan*,
the oiled paper floor.

Sometimes we listened to Haraboji's stories,
with Mother laughing hard,
clutching her sides,
and me laughing hard, too,
to see her so happy.

Sometimes we played *hato*,
a game of cards
with pictures of flowers and deer
and hills and the moon.
Mother would slap the cards down,
shouting when she won.

And always, every evening,
Imo would find some quiet
and we would sit close,
reading her book together,
until we went to sleep.

This was how they passed the time
with us

and this was how we passed the time
with them

until the day came
to make our trip back home—

and Haraboji gave us
a charcoal drawing
of the hills behind the house,

and Halmoni gave us
dried persimmons strung together
in a necklace,

and Imo gave us
a poem in Korean,
folded small—

and we gave them hugs.

and we gave them hugs.

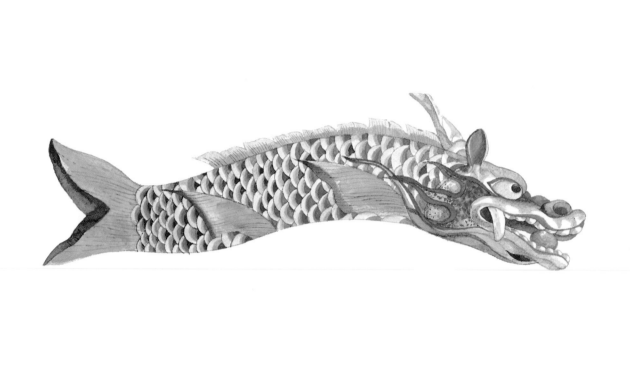